THE FAKE-CHICKEN KUNG FU FIGHTING BLUES

Aaron Lam

Illustrated by
Kean Soo

JAMES LORIMER & COMPANY LTD., PUBLISHERS
TORONTO

James Lorimer & Company Ltd., Publishers acknowledges funding support from the Ontario Arts Council (OAC), an agency of the Government of Ontario. We acknowledge the support of the Canada Council for the Arts, which last year invested $153 million to bring the arts to Canadians throughout the country. This project has been made possible in part by the Government of Canada and with the support of the Ontario Media Development Corporation.

Cover design: Tyler Cleroux and Kean Soo
Cover illustration: Kean Soo

Library and Archives Canada Cataloguing in Publication

Lam, Aaron, author
        The fake-chicken kung fu fighting blues / Aaron Lam ; illustrated by Kean Soo.

Issued in print and electronic formats.
ISBN 978-1-4594-1272-9 (softcover).--ISBN 978-1-4594-1273-6 (EPUB)

        I. Soo, Kean, illustrator II. Title

PS8623.A4655F35 2018   jC813'.6   C2017-906489-4
                                                                          C2017-906490-8

Published by:
James Lorimer &
Company Ltd., Publishers
117 Peter Street, Suite 304
Toronto, ON, Canada
M5V 0M3
www.lorimer.ca

Distributed in Canada by:
Formac Lorimer Books
5502 Atlantic Street
Halifax, NS, Canada
B3H 1G4

Distributed in the US by:
Lerner Publisher Services
1251 Washington Ave. N.
Minneapolis, MN, USA
55401
www.lernerbooks.com

Printed and bound in Canada.
Manufactured by Friesens Corporation in Altona, Manitoba, Canada in December 2017.
Job # 239695

For Erin and Laura. They rock.

CONTENTS

1

CHINATOWN FOREVER

I should have been spending less time with Jackson. He was the biggest dork in the world. Hanging out with him meant trouble. Besides, we were only twelve years old — and that was waaaay too young for jail!

My fingers were freezing, but I didn't want to put my phone down. I was getting awesome video footage of two fish kissing. Yep. You heard that right. The fish were kissing.

My buddy Jackson was holding two big fish, one in each hand. His gloves were getting slimier by the second, which was totally grossing me out. At the same time, I couldn't stop giggling at the puckering sounds he was making with his lips.

"Mmmppppaaaa! Mpppplhpmmmpuhhh!"

Like I said — a perfect shot. I'd been wandering around shooting video. No script. No director. Just me and my phone. I was capturing the sights and sounds of Chinatown. Then I ran into Jackson outside of Old Man Chan's fish market. Always the class clown, Jackson had started to perform what he called a "fish soap opera." Fresh fish from a plastic bin in front of the market ended up being his actors.

Then Old Man Chan showed up. And he wasn't happy with what he saw. Come to think of it, I don't think he was *ever* happy. We called him "Old Man" because his face was scrunched up like an old piece of leather. And he didn't have any teeth, which made his mouth look like a sinkhole. We were pretty sure he was over a hundred years old.

Poor Jackson didn't see Old Man Chan coming up behind him. He kept going with

ON A TYPICAL DAY IN CHINATOWN, ANTHONY AND JACKSON MAKE TROUBLE

the fish-kissing action. I stopped shooting, but Jackson didn't notice.

"Mmmmpuuuuuuh!"

Old Man Chan cleared his throat. Jackson froze. An expression of terror appeared on his face.

"Always the troublemaker," said Old Man Chan in Chinese. "Would you care to explain what's going on here?"

Jackson slowly turned to face his judge/jury/executioner.

"Hi, Old Man . . . I mean, Mr. Chan," said Jackson. His face turned bright red. "Would you believe this is for a school project?"

"Not for a minute!" replied Old Man Chan. His eyes ping-ponged between the two of us. "Both of you should get out of here before I call the police. Or worse — your moms!"

Jackson gently laid the fish back onto the ice. Then he bolted down the street. I politely smiled at Old Man Chan and went on my way.

In a few minutes, my phone buzzed. Jackson was texting to see if I'd survived my encounter with Old Man Chan. "Barely" was my response. "LOL" was his response to my response.

I took my time on my walk home, soaking in the exciting sights and sounds. Right in the heart of Toronto, Chinatown was filled with restaurants, bakeries, and markets. Souvenir shops everywhere sold the cheesiest "Welcome to Canada" trinkets you could imagine. I've heard people say that Chinatown is too noisy, but I never really thought of it that way. Chinatown always sounded *alive*, never ready to call it quits for the day — or night.

In case you hadn't figured it out yet, I loved Chinatown. I grew up there. I had the perfect life within its crazy streets. I would have laughed at the idea of leaving it. But that never even crossed my mind.

2

HOME, SWEET HOME

Our house was on a narrow street near Spadina Avenue, one of the main roads in the neighbourhood. Ours was a small, old house, but it was home. Five of us lived there: me (the one and only Anthony Chung), Mom, Dad, my grandmother, and my older sister Chloe. Chloe is only two years older than I am, but she likes to remind me that she's ten times smarter.

I'd barely made it through the front door. I didn't even have time to catch my breath before I heard a voice. "Did you forget your gloves again?" It was Chloe, yelling at me without even looking up from the TV. "I don't know why Mom and Dad bother buying you such nice winter clothes! When I was your age blah blah blah blah blah . . ."

I just tuned her out. She was the single most annoying human being on the planet — probably because she was so good at everything. Chloe was a straight-A student and the most popular kid at school. She was also good at every sport ever invented.

"Keep it down!" an annoyed voice shouted in Chinese from upstairs. "And turn down that TV!"

Grandma Peng, who we called "Po Po," thought we were spoiled brats. She had a growling voice that sounded like a landslide, along with an impressively ancient face. If Old Man Chan looked like he was a hundred years old, Po Po looked like she was a *thousand*. Imagine a cross between a rhinoceros and a prune. I know. Scary stuff.

Po Po had never spoken a word of English in her life. Ever since she moved to Chinatown from Hong Kong many moons ago, she never had any reason to learn English. Everyone here spoke her language. I could talk to Po Po because I spoke Chinese too. But I avoided her as much as I could because she was always complaining about something.

And that's exactly what she was doing that day. The day that turned out to be The Absolute Number One Worst Day in My Whole Entire Life.

I was texting with Jackson when a sudden pounding on my bedroom door made me jump.

"I'm studying!" I yelled. I thought it was my sister trying to annoy me.

The knocking continued, only harder this time.

"I said I'm studying! Go away!"

"Is that any way to talk to your Po Po?" It was angry Chinese coming from the other side of the door. "Don't your parents teach you any respect?"

Oops. "Sorry, Po Po. I thought you were Chloe."

"Well, can I come in or not?"

"Sorry," I said again. It was better to be safe than sorry. "I was just texting Jackson. Please come in."

Po Po opened the door. She came in and took a seat on the edge of my bed. It was strange that she would venture into my room at all. She often complained that it smelled like dirty socks. I was expecting some more scolding about not having respect. Or maybe about spending too much time on my phone texting Jackson. But it never came. Instead, she started crying.

"What's wrong, Po Po?" I asked. "Was it something I did?"

She looked at me and smiled. What a rare sight. "Of course not," she said. "I'm just sad that we'll be moving. I don't want to leave."

I couldn't believe my ears. "We're moving? What are you talking about?"

Po Po's eyes widened. "They never told you?"

They? I was more confused than ever.

Po Po just shook her head. "Your mother and father should have told you. We'll be moving in a few weeks."

The thought of leaving the house was like science-fiction. I'd lived there my whole life. All of my friends lived nearby. What were Mom and Dad thinking?

"Po Po, why are we moving? We're all happy here."

"I think I've said too much already. I'm sure they'll explain everything tonight."

Then she was gone.

I was left alone in my room with no answers and another hour before my parents came home from work.

My phone buzzed. It was Jackson again. He always texted me whenever he was bored, which was most of the time.

JACKSON: I'm bored. You want to come over and play video games?

ME: Nope. Not in the mood.

JACKSON: I just found an awesome new skateboarding video on YouTube. I'll send you the link.

ME: Don't bother. Not in the mood.

JACKSON: Dude, what's wrong?

ME: Everything, I think.

3

THE WORLD UPSIDE-DOWN

I was waiting as Mom and Dad walked through the door. One look and they could tell I wasn't exactly the happiest person in the world. They asked me and Chloe to join them in the living room. "Your Dad and I have something important to tell you," Mom said. She had the sense to hesitate a bit.

"Is it good news?" asked Chloe. She clearly didn't get the memo from Po Po. "Did we win the lottery?"

Mom cleared her throat. "We're moving. Right after Christmas."

Chloe looked stunned. I could count on one

hand the number of times I saw her speechless.

"How do you kids feel about that?" Mom asked.

Chloe finally spoke up. "Where are we going?"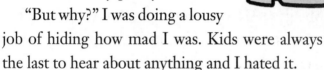

"To a small town in Northern Ontario. It's called Berksburg. And from what I've seen of it online, it's really pretty."

"But why?" I was doing a lousy job of hiding how mad I was. Kids were always the last to hear about anything and I hated it.

"The magazine is downsizing. I need to find another job," said Dad.

That was a huge shock to me. He'd worked at the magazine for as long as I could remember.

"But why this 'Burgerburg' place?" asked Chloe.

"*Berks*burg," Mom said.

"Yeah, whatever. But why?"

"We've known about this move for a few weeks now," Dad continued. "Your mother and I already have jobs lined up in Berksburg."

I couldn't imagine my parents working at different jobs. Or all of us living in a different town. It felt like a nightmare I just wanted to wake up from.

"I've found a job as the art director of the newspaper up there," he explained. "Your mother will be teaching at the high school."

Chloe leapt to her feet with a sudden burst of excitement. "That's fantastic!" she shouted. She gave Mom and Dad enormous hugs. "That sounds like so much fun! I can't wait to start packing!"

What? I couldn't believe Chloe. Couldn't she see what a disaster this was? I stomped back to my bedroom and slammed the door behind me.

Thus ended The Absolute Number One Worst Day in My Whole Entire Life. Things could only get better. Or so I hoped.

I spent the next few days online doing research about Berksburg. The town's official website looked ancient, like it was made during the early days of the Internet. The graphics were really out of date and half the links didn't work. The ones that *did* work led to really boring pages about the area's natural beauty. Trees, wildlife, and stuff like that.

I couldn't care less about trees and wildlife! I was a city boy. I wanted to know about the best places to shop for comic books and video games. I wanted to know about the best places to get good Chinese food. I wanted to know where the best movie theatres were playing the latest blockbusters.

The weeks sped by and moving day came too quickly. I looked around after I'd packed up my stuff. It was the first time I'd ever seen my bedroom completely empty. The sight made me realize I couldn't avoid reality forever. We were moving from the best city in the world to the most boring town in the universe. Yuck!

The movers arrived and started loading our furniture and boxes into the back of their huge truck. Some of Dad's old friends had a moving business and they'd agreed to lend their services. The guys were sweating like crazy, but they still looked half-frozen.

Jackson dropped by to say goodbye. We promised to keep in touch. But I wondered how long it would take before he forgot about me.

"We can still play video games together online," he said in a depressed voice. "And I'll still send you links to funny videos."

Jackson was always sending me links to videos that would make me laugh so hard I'd fall out of my chair. At least I could look forward to that — when the chairs were off the truck.

"Stay out of trouble," I said. I knew that he'd ignore my advice anyway. "And say hi to Old Man Chan for me when you see him again!"

It was time to set off for our new home. We piled into the family SUV and hit the road with the moving van following behind us. It was strange seeing our house grow smaller and smaller through the rear window.

Soon, Chinatown was behind us and we were on the highway

to the northern wastelands of Ontario. I really didn't know much about Berksburg, but I was expecting to see a lot of igloos and polar bears.

As we continued driving north, all signs of our previous life started to vanish. Before long, even the CN Tower shrank into the horizon behind us. All signs of city living started disappearing, replaced by rolling farmland and the occasional cow or horse.

A few hours into our drive, even the farmland was disappearing, replaced by forests of tiny pine trees that poked up through the rocky ground.

Occasionally we'd pass a group of kids playing shinny on a frozen pond. Shinny — what a stupid and pointless game! I never understood the national fascination with all things "hockey."

The next thing I remembered was waking up with a major crick in my neck. I must have dozed off. Mom was gently shaking my shoulder from the front seat.

"We're here, honey," she whispered.

"I told you it would be great," Dad said. "The fresh air. The peace and quiet. Very nice."

"This place is totally awesome!" shouted Chloe. She was like a cheerleader on a sugar high. "Awesome! Awesome! Awesome!"

Po Po was awakened briefly by the fuss. She just grunted. Then she closed her eyes and resumed her snorefest.

I rubbed the sleep out of my eyes and tried to focus on my surroundings. We were parked in front of a big white house with a porch that wrapped around one side. I was surprised at the size of the front lawn. It was as big as the local park back in Toronto. This place was a lot bigger than our old house, which didn't have a porch or a front lawn at all.

The moving truck pulled into the driveway behind us. Wow — we had a driveway now. We'd always struggled to find a parking spot on our street in Chinatown.

Everything was different. Strange.

"Welcome to Berksburg," Dad said. "We're home."

4

WHAT PLANET AM I ON?

Po Po was freaking out. One minute she was snoring happily and the next she was out of the car. She looked like a boxer ready for action. I had no idea what was going on, but that was usually the case when it came to Grandma.

"This is totally unacceptable!" she yelled in Chinese. She seemed to be talking to no one and everyone at the same time. Po Po's voice sounded harsh even when she was happy. It was downright scary when she was mad. I fought a strong urge to go running for the hills. This was the wilderness. There had to be hills.

Po Po pointed a crooked finger right at

Dad's nose. "What are you trying to do? Bring bad luck to this family? Why didn't anybody tell me about the house before we decided to come here?"

Mom and Dad looked confused. They clearly had no idea why Po Po was so angry. When she saw their puzzled faces, she became even *angrier*.

"Didn't you notice *that* over there?" she asked. She pointed to the railway tracks that ran through the field across the street. "You couldn't ask for worse luck!"

I could tell from the blank looks that no one understood what she was talking about.

"You should never have railway tracks in front of your house!" Po Po explained. "It represents the centipede. And the centipede will bring misfortune upon the family. We need a chicken!"

I started to laugh. A chicken? What was she talking about?

"This isn't funny, young man," Po Po barked at me. "We need a chicken to place over the front door. That's what my parents would have done, and their parents before them."

Then I started to understand why Po Po was freaking out. This was about Chinese tradition and old beliefs.

"A fake chicken will do," she continued. "Just like the ones you can buy in Chinatown. The chicken will protect the house by scaring the centipede away."

Po Po was superstitious. Super superstitious. She always took her ancient beliefs seriously. Sometimes she would move furniture around to avoid bad luck. Or she would take down a mirror because it was facing the wrong direction.

"Po Po, I don't think we'll be able to find a fake chicken in this town," I said.

"We must find one," she replied. "We *must*. If this family is to prosper, things must start off right. The foundation must be stable if what we build upon it is to be strong."

Dad put his hand on Po Po's shoulder in a vain attempt to calm her down. "We can look for a chicken on the Internet," he suggested.

"Oh yeah," said Chloe sarcastically. "I'm sure they have a category for 'fake chickens' on eBay."

I pulled out my phone so I could start looking online. I really wanted to know if I could find a rubber chicken for sale online. But I couldn't get a wireless signal. I suddenly panicked. If I couldn't get online, what was I going to do for fun around here?

I snapped back to reality. Po Po was still ranting about chickens and centipedes.

Mom was fighting to stay calm. But I could see she was getting mad too. "We can't always live by the old beliefs," she told Po Po. "We live in a modern world now. We shouldn't live in the past."

Po Po didn't respond. She was too busy looking for more things to complain about.

The movers had everything loaded into the house within a couple of hours. Then it was a matter of

YOU DON'T SELL FAKE CHICKENS, DO YOU?

?

NO, JACKSON. A *FAKE* CHICKEN.

GEEZ, ANTHONY. YOU REALLY *CAN* FIND ANYTHING ONLINE, CAN'T YOU?

unpacking and finding new places for every-thing. I wasn't in the mood to do anything but whine, but I forced myself to open my first box. The sooner I got started, the sooner I'd be finished.

I was really happy when Mom finally set up our wireless connection that night. At least I could surf the Internet and play online video games. My phone buzzed. A text from Jackson!

JACKSON: Wuzzup dude? Are you having fun yet? See any polar bears yet?

ME: No polar bears. Not a lot of fun, either. What are you up to?

JACKSON: Just got back from the mall. Bought a couple of video games. Going to see a movie tonight. What are you doing?

I'd never felt more homesick. Shopping at the mall. Buying video games. Seeing a movie.

That's what I loved about Toronto — there was so much to do.

Jackson's text stared back at me. "What are you doing?"

ME: Absolutely nothing.

JACKSON: LOL. Gotta go. I don't want to miss the movie. Later.

I sat in my room and sulked. I hated how quiet everything was here. In Toronto, I could always hear honking cars and police sirens. Excitement. Adventure. I closed my eyes and thought about the crazy adventures I always had with Jackson. It almost felt like I was back in the city . . .

Bam! Bam! I was jolted awake by knocking on my door. It was Dad.

"Anthony, I guess we never had a chance to talk about moving," he said. He sat on the edge of my bed. "I know this is hard on you. I'm sorry we didn't tell you earlier."

"I'm feeling really confused," I said. To my

surprise, I really *did* want to talk. "Can I ask you a few questions?"

"Go ahead."

I started shooting questions at a rapid-fire pace.

"Are there any Chinese restaurants in Berksburg?"

"I'm not sure."

"Are there any other Chinese kids in Berksburg?"

"I don't know."

"Are there any other Chinese people in Berksburg?"

"Maybe."

"Is there a movie theatre in Berksburg?"

"No. It's too small."

"What do people do here for fun?"

"I don't have the slightest idea."

Our little game of Twenty Questions ended up involving a lot more than twenty questions. The answers weren't making me feel any better, so I eventually stopped asking. Dad went back to unpacking.

I didn't sleep well that night, but at least it was only Saturday. I wouldn't be starting class until Monday. Sunday would be my day of exploration, a chance to take my first bold steps into a brave new world. That was the idea, anyway.

5

FIRST STEPS

When morning came, I bundled up and ventured into the great unknown. Not a lot of other houses shared our quiet road, which made me miss the excitement of Chinatown even more. I was surrounded by evergreen trees and rocks. Borrrrrrring.

A movement in the distance suddenly caught my attention. Something was in the field across the road. It was a deer! I'd never seen one with my own eyes before.

The deer lifted its head. It became very alert, sensing something in the air. In the blink of an eye, it leaped off through the brush and beyond my sight. I hoped it didn't run away because of me.

Then I realized why the deer had sped off. There was a coyote on the prowl. It limped in pursuit of the deer for only a few steps before giving up the chase. I saw that one of its front legs was missing. Running at high speed was no longer possible for the poor guy.

The coyote turned to face me, then started trotting in my direction. Fascination quickly turned into fear. I was too young to be eaten by a wild animal! When I swung around to start running, I crashed headlong into someone. We both toppled into the snow with a loud thud.

"Watch where you're going!" shouted an angry voice as we stumbled to our feet and brushed ourselves off. The voice was from a redheaded boy. He was about my age, only a lot taller, a lot broader, and a lot angrier. He picked up the hockey stick and puck that he'd dropped. Beside him was a cute girl. She was my age too, with reddish-blonde hair and amazing dark eyes.

"I'm really sorry," I said, still half-dazed. "I was running . . ."

"Running? Running from what?" asked the boy, whose anger was quickly cooling.

"That!" I replied, pointing in the direction of the charging coyote. They looked confused, probably because the coyote was nowhere to be seen.

"Are you okay?" asked the girl.

"Yeah, but there was a coyote coming this way. It had only three legs, but it looked really hungry."

She laughed. "You saw Clark."

"Clark?"

"Let's go," said the boy. "This kid doesn't even know who Clark is. Everybody knows Clark."

"I'm new here," I replied. "That coyote has a name?"

The big guy turned. He headed down the road without even a glance back. "You can stay and chat if you want," he said to the girl. "But I'm going."

"Charming, isn't he?" she said to me. "See you later."

Then she was gone too. So I continued my mission of exploration.

I could tell that I'd arrived downtown when I reached the only set of traffic lights in Berksburg. Small shops and restaurants lined Main Street, but nothing was open. One diner had a poster in its window advertising THE BEST SUBMARINE SANDWICH FOR 100 MILES.

Probably the only submarine sandwich for a hundred miles, I thought. Maybe my standards for fast food would have to be adjusted.

As I made my way alongside the river that ran through town, I heard the distant sounds of slashing hockey sticks and skates scraping on ice. The commotion grew louder as I approached a steep hill along the riverbank. When I reached the top of the rise, I saw three large ponds, each one crowded with people playing shinny.

I could never understand the appeal of shinny, or "pond hockey" as it's known outside

of Canada. Nobody in my family was ever interested in the game. Maybe it was because we
never saw Chinese hockey players on TV.

"Dude, can you throw us the puck?"

It took me a second to realize that the voice
was speaking to me.

"Dude! The puck!"

I saw that a puck had landed in the snow just
a few paces from me on the hill. When I stepped
forward to retrieve it, I found myself slipping
on an icy patch. I tumbled down the hill like a
bowling ball. My body finally came to rest at
the edge of the pond when I hit a snowbank
face-first. Several kids came running over to the
accident scene.

"Are you okay?"

I cleared the snow from my eyes. I saw
through a fluffy, white mask that the
voice had come from the
same girl I'd met earlier
with the amazing dark eyes.
I started brushing snow off vari-
ous body parts. When it was

clear I wasn't (seriously) hurt, several people burst into laughter at my clumsiness.

At least the girl didn't laugh. She just smiled. Hopefully it was warmth she was trying to show and not pity.

"Well, well, well." That voice was familiar too. I winced when I saw that it came from the redheaded boy I'd tackled earlier. "If it isn't the boy who always falls."

My immediate reaction was an overwhelming desire to sling some snow into his face. But I valued my life too much to follow through. He was quite a bit bigger than me.

"So where's my puck?" he asked. Unlike the others, he was obviously not concerned about my well-being. Even after seeing my death-defying tumble off a cliff.

"He caught it while he was rolling," said the girl. "It was an impressive move."

I was shocked to see the puck clutched in my right hand. Hmm. Maybe I had a future as a goalie. Without saying a word, I tossed the puck to Big Red. He plucked it from the air and went back to his game with the rest of his gang. Only the girl stayed to help me up from the snow.

"Don't mind him," she said. "He's got a one-track mind. Can't think of anything except for hockey. I'm Lise Laurier, by the way."

I shook her hand cautiously, still a bit surprised by her friendliness. And at how pretty her eyes were. "Um, hi," I sputtered. "My name's Anthony."

"Do you like hockey too?" she asked. "It was amazing how you caught that puck as you rolled down the hill. You grabbed it from the air in the middle of your ninja flip."

She was putting quite a positive spin on things. I wasn't going to argue with her. "That's what I was going for."

"Lise!" came that annoying boy's voice again. "Can you throw us the puck?" This time the stupid thing had become lodged in a snowbank. Lise quickly retrieved it so the game could continue.

"Your boyfriend's quite the gentleman," I said.

She looked confused. "My boyfriend?"

"Yeah, the hockey-playing hunk over there."

She just smiled and shook her head. "That's not my boyfriend. That's my brother Marty. We're twins."

I was more than a little happy to hear that he wasn't her boyfriend. Maybe there *was* some justice in the world after all. "Twins, eh? At least you aren't as ugly as he is!"

Lise didn't laugh at my joke. I wasn't sure if I'd offended her. Feeling like a dork, I knew I had to get out of there as quickly as I could.

"Bye!" was all I could manage before I dashed off.

6

PRAYING MANTIS KUNG FU

The first day of school. I always hated those dreaded words. It always meant one thing — freedom had come to an end.

I was a nervous wreck as I approached the schoolyard. I took a deep breath and tried to look confident. "Keep your chin up and never let them see you sweat," I muttered into the video journal I kept on my phone. "And stop talking to yourself out loud. People are giving you weird looks."

Berksburg Central was a lot bigger than my old school in Chinatown. The schoolyard alone was huge, with its football field, baseball diamond, and running track. My old school didn't have any grass at all and the schoolyard was just a small patch of concrete.

I was still getting weird looks from everyone (and I wasn't even talking to myself anymore). It was clear that I was the new kid in town. I stuck out like a sore thumb.

Then I heard a familiar voice coming from behind me. I turned around to see Lise chatting with a couple of her friends. She hadn't noticed me yet.

I was just about say "hi" when I felt a strong hand clamp down on my shoulder.

"Well, well, well," said the only other familiar voice in Berksburg that wasn't from my family. "If it ain't the Human Snowball himself!"

I turned around slowly to face Marty. He had an icy grin that terrified me.

"Good morning," I squeaked. "Beautiful day, huh?"

Marty tightened his grip on my shoulder and it started to hurt. "Why are you so interested in

my sister?" he asked. His grin was suddenly gone.

"Leave him alone, Marty!" I heard Lise say from behind me.

"I'm not bothering him," he replied. "I just wanted to ask him a question. Because nobody talks to my sister without going through me first."

"I don't need a bodyguard!" she said. I was glad her frown wasn't directed at me.

The big guy tightened his grasp even more, making me wince. He leaned in closer and looked directly into my soul with his steely eyes. "That's my twin sister. And it's my job to look after her. You got that?"

Then a large and meaty hand, even larger and meatier than Marty's, landed on his shoulder with a thud. Marty released his grip on me. He spun around to see who had interrupted our little conversation.

A monstrous kid, a few heads taller than Marty and a whole

lot heavier, towered over all of us. With a long mop of greasy hair framing a rough-and-tumble face, the giant did not look happy at all. He was munching loudly on handfuls of potato chips he was scooping from a jumbo bag.

"Hi, Buck," said Marty. He sounded about as scared and wimpy as I had just moments before. It was weird to hear Marty's voice quivering.

"I forgot my lunch," said Buck in a voice that was inhumanly deep. "That means I've got to buy lunch today. But I forgot my lunch money too. Give me all your money and I'll let you go without a knuckle sandwich. Understand?"

Lise had her fists balled up tightly. She looked ready to jump in and protect her brother. Maybe it was my protective instinct, or maybe it was my deep hatred of bullies, but I had to do something.

"Let him go, Big Buck!" I blurted. I was surprised at the amount of authority in my squeaky voice.

Buck released his hold on Marty and grabbed me by the collar.

"Did you just call me 'Big Buck,' little fella?" he asked. His face was turning impressively red. "Nobody calls me that. Now you'll pay the price too."

Marty was so shocked at the turn of events that he seemed paralyzed. I guess I wasn't going to get any help from him.

"Not so fast, bonehead!" I shouted, doing my best impersonation of an action hero. "Leave us alone, or you'll have to face the fury of the Chinese praying mantis!"

Lise and Marty stared at me in confusion. They clearly wondered what strategy I was using to (hopefully) prevent my doom. To be honest, I wasn't completely sure myself.

Buck didn't seem very frightened by my threat. "Praying mantis, huh? I suppose you're gonna tell me you know karate or something like that?"

"Not karate," I said. I tried to lower the tone of my voice to sound cooler. "Karate is kids' play. I'm talking about praying-mantis-style kung fu, the deadliest in the world!"

The bully still didn't seem that impressed. "Really? And I suppose a little runt like you is gonna give me a demonstration of this deadly kung fu?"

He'd called my bluff. I didn't know kung fu in the slightest. Not wanting to reveal any weakness, I started moving my arms and legs in the slow, rhythmic motions of tai chi. This came naturally, thanks to regular lessons from Po Po.

"Is that supposed to scare me?" Buck was barely able to suppress his laughter.

My tai chi moves couldn't scare a kitten. I needed to do something dramatic. So I kicked into the air and yelled like a crazy man, "YAAAAHHHHHH!"

One of my boots flew off my foot. It shot straight into Buck's nose. Down he went.

Everyone was too shocked to do or say anything, Buck included.

After a few moments of groaning in the snow, Buck stumbled to his feet and struggled to regain his breath. "All right! You win. Just stay away from me with that praying-mantis kung fu stuff."

Then he hurried off, wanting nothing more to do with us.

"Wow," was all I could muster.

"Wow," said Lise and Marty in unison.

It was only when my socked foot started feeling numb from the cold that I snapped back to reality. I recovered my boot and shook out all the snow. As I was lacing up, another hand clamped down on my shoulder. Now what?

I spun around and came face to face with Marty. To my surprise, he had a warm smile that actually made him look friendly.

"Thanks for saving my butt," he said. This time his voice was gentle. I hardly recognized it. "Buck is the biggest bully in town. And he usually gets whatever he wants. What's your name again?"

"Anthony," I replied. Was this how quickly an enemy could become a friend? "Nice to meet you, Marty."

"You've gotta teach me some of those fancy kung fu moves of yours!" he said with a sudden burst of excitement.

I had to be honest. "Actually, I don't know any kung fu."

"You're joking!"

"Nope. I don't know kung fu. What I did was tai chi. It's a form of exercise I do to help me relax before bed. My Grandma taught me."

Marty stared at me, speechless. Then Lise started giggling, which got Marty laughing too.

7

EVERYTHING
HOCKEY!

The first day of school wasn't bad at all. My teachers and classmates were really friendly, which calmed my nerves right away. And it was nice that Lise and Marty were both in my class.

Chloe and I seemed to be the only Chinese kids in town. But my class was pretty diverse for being in the middle of nowhere. Joe's family was from Kenya and Elena was from Argentina. Both of them seemed happy and they had a lot of friends. Maybe I'd adapt to life here too.

I was surprised to learn that Berksburg had a Chinese restaurant, which was called Golden Egg Roll. The restaurant was first opened by a Chinese family many years ago, but they had since moved away. The current owners of Golden Egg Roll were from Jamaica, and they served a combination of Chinese and Jamaican cuisine. I couldn't imagine what kind of dishes they had on their menu. Apparently their food was pretty good. Lise and Marty promised to take me there sometime soon.

When classes were over, I was exhausted and eager to go home so I could collapse on my bed.

"You're joining us at the ponds again tonight, right?" asked Marty as we bundled up for the walk home.

"I don't know," I said while trying to hide a yawn. "I'm kinda tired and . . ."

Lise took me by the arm. That got my attention. "Everybody's going be there," she said. "Let's just go and hang out for a while."

I looked into Lise's dark brown eyes. I just couldn't say no. My folks wouldn't be too upset if I came home a bit late, especially if they knew I was doing my best to fit in and make new friends.

The ponds were already full of people when we arrived. Little kids, teenagers, adults, and even seniors were skating around. Many of them were playing their own games of shinny on their own patches of ice. It looked like most of the town was here.

"You guys really like your hockey!" I said in amazement.

"Of course we do!" Marty blurted. He looked shocked that I'd make such an obvious statement. "Hockey *is* Canada. Canada *is* hockey. Everybody loves hockey!"

I didn't, but I wasn't about to say that out loud.

"I never cared much for the game myself," admitted Lise. It must have taken guts to say that, especially in Berksburg. "I don't understand why people get so excited about it."

She was a girl after my own heart.

"Do you have your own skates, Anthony?" asked Marty. "You can join us in a game any time."

"Of course I have my own skates," I said, lying through my teeth. "I have them packed away in a box somewhere. I'll look for them tonight." Truth be told, I hadn't skated for years. And I was never very good at it. On top of that, I'd never actually held a hockey stick before.

Suddenly Marty was bellowing at the top of his lungs, "Does anybody have an extra pair of skates and a stick my friend can borrow?"

Within seconds, I was offered my choice of three pairs of skates (including a pink pair of toddler skates) and a hockey stick. So much for my excuse not to play! One pair of skates was a pretty good fit, so at least they wouldn't go flying off my feet like my boot had.

Soon Marty and I were both laced up and ready to hit the ice.

"Aren't you joining us?" I asked Lise as she took a seat on a nearby log.

"No thanks," she said. "Hockey really isn't my thing. I'm more into soccer. And basketball. And curling."

Marty just laughed. "That's my sis, all right. One of the best athletes in school. Dominates every sport she plays. But she doesn't like hockey. That's weird considering how good she is with a stick and puck. I don't know what's wrong with her!"

Lise stuck her tongue out playfully. "There's nothing wrong with me, thank you very much!"

I slowly sauntered my way onto the ice using the hockey stick like a third leg. My ankles wouldn't stop wobbling. I wanted desperately to look like a cool athlete in front of Lise. But clearly that was not to be.

After a few clumsy strides, I fell onto my bum with a spectacular "wham." *Ouch!* My fall was greeted by a chorus of laughter from every direction. I wondered to myself: *Is hockey for a Chinese kid like me?* Maybe I should have sat this one out.

Marty was quick to help me up from the cold ice. "You're not exactly an ace on skates, are you?"

I didn't want to look him in the eyes.

"Actually, I've never played hockey before."

The crowd at the pond gave a collective gasp. I looked over at Lise to see her reaction. She just smiled at me with those warm, sparkling eyes.

Then I looked up at Marty. Weird — I couldn't detect any trace of disappointment on his face. I was half-expecting him to disown me, and we hadn't even been friends for a full day yet!

"No problem," he said. "We can teach you how to play if you'd like. I don't know if you've noticed, but pretty much everything here in Berksburg revolves around hockey."

"Yeah, I noticed," I said sheepishly. "Maybe I should start heading home. My parents will be expecting me for dinner."

Marty gave me a hearty pat on the back. "Suit yourself, but the offer stands. If you ever want hockey lessons from the best hockey player in town, just ask me."

8

NEW FRIENDS AND OLD FEARS

Dinner was interesting. We had takeout from Golden Egg Roll. As advertised, the food was a strange mix of Chinese and Jamaican cooking. It was unlike anything I'd ever tasted. The jerk-chicken wonton soup wasn't half bad, but the curry-goat chow mein was just plain odd.

I was tired from a busy day, so it felt good to crash on my bed after dinner. The thought of hiding in my room and getting some peace and quiet sounded good to me.

Then Dad started shouting.

"Where's my video camera?" His frustrated voice echoed down the hallway.

"Why does everyone keep taking it? This is ridiculous!"

I just wanted to play video games and watch movies on my tablet. But I couldn't drown out the commotion coming from my parents' room. Dad was in one of his moods and he wanted to let the whole world know it. I could hear him opening and closing cardboard box lids in the loudest way possible. Cardboard usually doesn't make much noise. But he managed to make an impressive racket.

"Where is that camera? That question was for you, Anthony!" Nothing annoyed Dad more than losing something. On top of that, he loved his video camera like a baby. "Anthony!"

"Dad! I'm trying to study!"

He stomped down the hallway and poked his head into my room. His face was beet red. Not a good sign. That meant his internal temperature was going up. I just hoped it wouldn't reach boiling point.

"My video camera. You had it last, didn't you?"

That was a silly question. Why would I want to use his stupid camcorder when I could shoot video on my phone? His camera was really big and heavy. And it had a million buttons. I tried reading the manual once and it made my head spin. Plus, the camera was five years old — what an antique!

"Professional filmmakers use *real* cameras like mine," he was fond of saying. "Shooting videos on your phone is for amateurs."

"Wasn't Chloe using your camera for something right before we moved?" I asked.

He paused to think for a moment. Then he turned and stomped toward my sister's room. "Chloe! What did you do with my video camera?"

I knew for a fact that Chloe didn't have Dad's camera. She had no interest in making videos. But at least it got Dad off my back and I could get back to my fun.

My phone buzzed. It was Jackson texting me.

JACKSON: Dude, I almost got killed by Old Man Chan again today.

ME: What happened? You don't want to mess with that guy! He's scary!

JACKSON: My mom sent me to his market to pick up some groceries. He chased me out of the store. Almost caught me too. I hid behind a dumpster for a while.

We sent a few messages back and forth until he had to go. Hearing about Old Man Chan made me miss the good old days. I scrolled through the video files on my phone and found the footage we'd shot in Chinatown of two fish kissing. Even though only a few weeks had passed, it felt like a lifetime ago. My old life was definitely gone.

"You miss it too." I jumped at the sound of the gravelly voice speaking in Chinese. Po Po was standing in my doorway.

"Sorry," she said. "I wanted to see how you were doing."

I was surprised to see how she looked. Po Po rarely looked happy, but I'd rarely seen her look this sad. She had the droopy expression of a bulldog on a rainy day.

"I'm doing fine," I said. "I'm making new friends at school already." (I didn't tell her about the new enemy I'd made too.)

"Good," she said, taking a seat on my bed. "It takes time to adjust."

"How are *you* doing, Po Po?"

She tried to force a smile, but it was pretty unconvincing. Maybe the whole smiling thing would work better if she got around to buying some teeth.

"I'm doing . . . fine," she said.

"Really?"

"No!" she blurted with frustration. She dropped her "happy" act abruptly. At least she wasn't doing that creepy smile thing anymore. "I don't speak English, so it's hard for me to make new friends here. I feel stuck in this house."

For the first time, I realized that Po Po hadn't left the house since we'd moved to

Berksburg. She was hiding from the world outside — hiding from her fears.

"You shouldn't feel stuck here," I told her.
"You should just bundle up and explore Berksburg.
It'll make you feel better. I can come with you."

Po Po just shook her head. "No, I don't
think I belong out there."

I turned off my phone and set it
aside. I gave Po Po my full attention,
but she changed the subject suddenly.

"What were you watching anyway?"
she asked.

"It was just an old video I shot for
school. I had to show why Chinatown
is so great. And there were these two
fish . . . I'll just show you. It's too hard to
explain."

When I showed her the video on my
phone, she didn't laugh a single time. Her sense
of humour was very different from mine. I don't
think she liked the video very much.

"Could you do the same thing for this place?"

I didn't understand what she was asking me.

"Could you make a video about Berksburg?" she continued. "To show what this town is all about. Then I could see more of this place without leaving the house."

"I guess I could," I replied. "Would that make you feel more comfortable here?"

"Yes."

If making a video would help Po Po, then it would be worth the effort. On top of that, it would give me a new reason to hang out at the ponds with Marty and Lise. Maybe I couldn't skate or play hockey, but I could film it.

"I'll show you that there's nothing to be scared of," I said. "I miss Chinatown too. But Berksburg isn't as bad as I expected. Maybe you'll like it too."

Po Po shook her head. "You're young and you can adapt," she replied. "I'm too old for change."

Dad poked his head into my room again. "I found the video camera!" he said with relief. "Just like I said — it was in one of my boxes all along!"

Soon, they both left me alone so I could enjoy my evening in peace. I started getting excited about making a video for Po Po. It would be fun to get Lise and Marty involved too. Mentally I started making space on my bookshelf for an Oscar.

9

YOU WOULDN'T BELIEVE IT UNLESS YOU SAW IT FOR YOURSELF

I made my way to the ponds. I knew most of the town's population would be gathering there on a sunny Saturday morning like this. Every centimetre of ice was crammed with people. Some of the kids on skates looked barely old enough to be walking. Other people looked way *too* old to be walking, much less skating. A couple of shinny players looked more ancient than Po Po, if that was even possible.

I quickly ran into Marty and Lise. They were both preparing to join a game.

"I thought you didn't 'get' hockey!" I said to Lise half-jokingly.

She just smiled. "I do it for the exercise. It's a great workout."

"Did you come for a hockey lesson?" Marty asked as he offered me his hockey stick.

"No thanks," I replied. "I'm here to make a video for my grandma."

"That sounds like fun," Lise said. "You should bring her to the ponds sometime."

"Yeah, but Grandma's too scared to leave the house."

"Why?" asked Marty. "There's nothing to be scared of."

I explained my reason for making the video. Right away, Marty and Lise wanted to be a part of it. They suggested that I film some of their shinny match. Once the camera on my phone was rolling, he started to demonstrate his awesome skills with a stick and puck. Lise was no slouch when it came to the game either. She was just as fast and fearless as her twin on the ice.

Marty scored one of his effortless-looking goals.

"I'm the king of the world!" He raised his arms in victory and shouted at the top of his lungs, still skating. Then Marty's left skate hit a bump in the ice. He flew into the air like a stunt car off a ramp. Spectators on the sidelines jumped for cover as Marty became Berksburg's version of Superman.

He smashed through an innocent snowman and began rolling like a bowling ball. He destroyed a snow fort before bouncing off a snowbank. Then he tumbled straight through a second snowman and went crashing into another snowbank headfirst. Only his legs were visible sticking straight up from the snow. He looked like a human popsicle.

"Please tell me you got that on camera," said Lise.

Marty managed to free himself from his icy prison. He was hailed by everyone as a hero for his spectacular stunt. People thought it was all done on purpose!

"Wow!" said one little boy who looked up at Marty in awe. "That was an amazing move!"

"It wasn't easy," Marty replied, playing along. "I meant to do that. Totally. I call that move 'The Pinball.' It took years of practice."

"Oh, brother!" said Lise.

"Again!" some of the younger kids started yelling.

"Sorry, little ones," said Mighty Marty. He was really enjoying the attention. "Only one show per day. It takes a lot out of you."

After all the excitement had died down, Marty, Lise, and I took a seat on a log and played back the day's footage on my phone.

"You're really good at shooting video!" said Lise.

I could feel myself turning red. I wasn't used to getting compliments on my work.

"Yeah, your stuff looks great!" said Marty. "Especially how you captured my amazing stunt! Did you see how I took out *two* snow-men? TWO!"

"Have you ever considered making a real

film?" asked Lise. "Not just a video for your Grandma, but a documentary about Berksburg."

I'd never really considered that, but the idea wasn't half bad.

"Hockey means everything to this town," said Marty. "It's always been in our blood."

"My brother's a real history nut," said Lise. "Especially when it comes to local hockey. He could help you with it."

Actually, it sounded like a lot of fun. Dad had some video-editing software on his laptop I could use.

Anthony the Documentary Filmmaker. I liked the sound of that.

"Hey, you!"

I recognized that deep, menacing voice right away.

"Hey! You're name's Anthony Chung, right?"

I turned around slowly. "Yeah, I'm Anthony."

Sure enough, it was Buck, the Big Bully of Berksburg. Was it possible that he was looking for a rematch? Was he planning to tear me apart with his bare hands?

"I'm sorry about picking on you the other day," Buck said. His voice was surprisingly soft. "I told my Dad what happened and he got mad at me. Bullying isn't cool."

My jaw dropped. I couldn't believe what I was hearing.

"Plus, my Dad said I couldn't have any more potato chips until I told you I was sorry. Apology accepted?" he asked.

"You bet!" Lise, Marty, and I answered with relief.

"Hey, Anthony, can you teach me kung fu?"

I hated stringing Buck along, so I had to be honest with him. "I'm going to tell you a secret, but you have to promise you won't get mad."

"Sure. I promise."

I took a deep breath. "I don't know kung fu at all. I was doing tai chi when my boot came off. Tai chi isn't a martial art. It's a meditation exercise."

Buck looked really confused. "But your flying-boot kick was so perfect!"

"Pure luck. I didn't mean to hit you. It was an accident."

All of a sudden, Buck started laughing hysterically. Then he gave me a friendly punch in the arm that was sure to leave a mark for a few days.

"Tai chi, huh?" Buck said. "Can you teach me that? It still looks pretty cool, whatever you call it."

"My grandma's the real expert," I said. "I don't know much more than you do."

"Then can your grandma teach me? I'd really like to learn."

Lise jumped in, "Yeah, me too."

I looked at Marty to see what he was thinking.

"Count me in too," he said.

Maybe this would be a good way to build up Po Po's confidence. At least she'd get to meet a few people outside of our family.

"Let me talk to my grandma about giving some tai chi lessons," I told them. I had the feeling this was going to be a win-win situation.

10

WHEN WORLDS COLLIDE

On my way home, I had the strange feeling that I was being watched from the woods. I stopped in my tracks and slowly looked over my shoulder. It was getting foggy, so I wasn't a hundred per cent sure that my eyes weren't playing tricks on me. But I thought I saw Clark the coyote. Then the vision vanished into the thickening fog.

Was he stalking me? Was he warning me to stay away from his territory? Was he thinking about eating me for lunch?

I wasn't superstitious like Po Po, but it was getting creepy. I felt like I was in a werewolf movie and the monster was going to jump out any minute. I listened to some music on my phone to calm my nerves, but it wasn't helping very much. My heart was beating fast and I found myself jogging instead of walking.

Luckily, I didn't encounter Clark again on my way home. Everyone said that Clark was harmless, but I didn't want to take my chances with a wild animal. Especially a *hungry* wild animal.

When I got home, I went straight to Po Po's room and knocked on her door.

"What do you want?" asked the cranky voice from the other side in Chinese.

"It's Anthony. Can I come in? There's something I want to ask you."

I heard an impatient sigh/grunt from inside her room. It sounded like a cross between a deflating balloon and a really grouchy dog. Not a nice sound.

When Po Po opened the door, I could see that she'd been crying. She was in no mood for company. I was tempted to run away as fast I could. But I stood my ground. I could do this.

"Po Po, can I ask you a question?"

She sighed/grunted again. It made the hairs on the back of my neck stand up — it was so unpleasant. "If you must."

"I have three friends who . . ."

"You have only *three* friends? Shouldn't you have more than three friends by now? Why aren't you getting to know more kids at school?"

"Please let me finish," I said. "I have three friends who are interested in learning tai chi. Can I bring them over so you can teach them?"

She turned white. "Me? But I can't speak English!"

"No problem. I'll be the translator!"

"But —"

"Thanks, Po Po! I'll bring them over tomorrow afternoon! You're the best!"

I turned and left for my room. The conversation had gone even better than expected. Another mission accomplished!

The tai chi lessons began the next day. I lined up on one side of the living room with Marty, Lise, and Buck. Facing us was Po Po, who looked more than a bit grumpy. I think she was still mad at me for making her do this. Or maybe she was feeling gassy from breakfast, which happened a lot.

We had lots of space for our lesson. According to feng shui, a house should always be free of clutter, so Po Po insisted that very little furniture be placed in the living room. Besides one couch, two chairs, and a bookshelf, the room was empty. Mom wanted to add a nice coffee table and a rocking chair to make the room feel more welcoming. But Po Po wouldn't allow it. She was convinced that the extra clutter would bring bad luck to the family.

"Tai chi involves slow, flowing movements to strengthen your body and mind," Po Po explained in Chinese. I translated into English for the others as she went on. "It's all about control."

"How did you learn tai chi, Mrs. Peng?" asked Lise.

"My late husband taught me," replied Po Po after I had translated the question for her. "It helped him reach a new level of inner peace and wisdom. Plus he thought it made him look cool. He said the ladies really dug it."

I wasn't sure how to translate that last bit, even if I'd wanted to. So I just left it out.

Po Po began to show us some basic tai chi moves and everyone managed to keep up. Even Buck looked elegant in motion.

Tai chi requires the whole body, not just the arms. It took all my concentration at times to avoid tripping over my own feet. Balance was never my strong suit and I found myself in danger of toppling over like a domino.

I was getting into a groove after a few minutes. Then I made the fatal mistake of looking around to see how the others were doing.

I fell over. I knocked over Marty, who knocked over Lise, who knocked over Buck.

Buck fell against the bookcase. The bookcase wobbled, and an expensive-looking vase fell off the top shelf.

What happened next seemed to unfold in slow motion:

1. Po Po slapped her forehead in disbelief. It was really loud.

2. Lise jumped for the vase in an attempt to catch it before it hit the ground.

3. Lise got her hands on the vase, but only for an instant. The vase slipped out of her hands and shot back into the air.

4. Lise kept flying in one direction while the vase flew in the opposite direction.

5. Lise tackled Buck with a thud.

6. Then it was Marty's turn to reach for the vase.

7. He caught it!

8. He smiled in triumph.

9. The vase slipped out of his hands.

10. The vase smashed into a hundred pieces on the floor.

We all looked at the mess in disbelief. That vase had been with our family for as long as I could remember. I hoped it wasn't a priceless antique or a valuable family heirloom. I also hoped it wasn't important to the feng shui of the room!

Po Po's mouth hung open in shock, revealing the toothless cavern of darkness within.

"Do you realize what you've just done?" Po Po asked in a quivering voice. I didn't need to translate.

"I'm so sorry," squeaked Marty.

"How can we make it up to you?" I asked.

"Make it up to me?" she responded. "Why would you need to make it up to me?"

She began to laugh. Okay, now I was confused.

"Anthony, your father gave that vase to me

as a birthday gift. He bought it at the corner store for about two bucks. I always thought it was ugly. But I never told your father because I didn't want to hurt his feelings. Now I don't have to look at it anymore. You and your friends have done me a favour by breaking it!"

I translated for the group. Marty sighed in relief. Lise started giggling. Buck was too shocked to react at all. Somehow, we'd survived our first tai chi lesson.

11

GETTING DOWN TO BUSINESS

It was time to get serious about making this film about Berksburg. I was surprised that Dad was letting me use his expensive video camera.

"I'm so proud that you want to be a film-maker," he said. "I always dreamed about winning an Academy Award. Maybe *you'll* win one someday!"

He showed me what all the buttons were for. I promised that I wouldn't drop or break his beloved camera. If any harm came to it, I'd be grounded for life!

My first step was to interview Marty and

Lise to get their thoughts. I was expecting Lise to be good on camera, but I didn't know how well Marty would do. He'd proven himself to be a man of action rather than a talker.

We picked a nice spot on the ridge over-looking the ponds so the camera would pick up the shinny action in the background. Marty was a bit nervous about being interviewed, so Lise decided to go first.

Actually, I was probably more nervous than Marty was. Being a serious interviewer was a totally new experience for me. I cleared my throat, straightened my back and started asking questions in my best TV-announcer voice.

Here are some highlights from my interview with Lise:

ME: What can you tell me about Berksburg?

LISE: Berksburg is all about hockey. You could say that Berksburg *is* hockey.

ME: What makes hockey so special here?

LISE: Hockey's a tradition passed down from generation to generation. That's why you see people of all ages playing shinny on the ponds. People in Berksburg learn to play the game shortly after they learn to walk.

ME: But you're not a big fan of hockey yourself, are you?

MARTY (his voice in the background):
BOOOOOOOOOOOO!

LISE (to Marty): Hey! Wait for your turn!

ME: As I was saying, you're not obsessed with hockey like everybody else around here. Why is that?

LISE: I'm not obsessed with hockey. But I can appreciate it for its cultural importance to Canadians.

MARTY (his voice in the background): She always has to complicate things! It's just an awesome game. Period.

LISE: Just ignore him. I appreciate hockey's rich history in this town, the athletic ability needed for the game, and the elegance of players in action.

ME: Wow. That's deep.

Then a volley of snowballs zoomed past me. Lise was plastered with wet snow from head to toe. She was not impressed. Marty was already preparing his next attack when Lise went on the offensive.

A snow battle of epic proportions unfolded. I made sure to capture it all on video. Marty was much quicker at making snowballs and getting them airborne, but Lise had better aim.

Half an hour later, the snow fight was still raging on. They weren't even slowing down. I waved goodbye and I started heading home. We could continue with the interviews another time.

Production on my epic motion picture continued over the next few weeks. It was handy having friends like Lise and Marty. They knew everybody in Berksburg and they helped me get some great interviews for the video.

Coming from a big city like Toronto, I thought it was weird that everyone in this town knew everybody else. Lise and Marty were related to half the people in Berksburg. The other half were either friends from school or friends of their family. Even though I hadn't been in town for that long, I already knew most of the people at the ponds. It felt nice not being a complete stranger any more.

Lise introduced me to the Berksburg Oldtymers, a team of female hockey players who'd been playing together for decades. The youngest member of the Oldtymers was sixty-two and the oldest was eighty-six. They could skate and shoot a puck better than people half their age!

The team captain, Gertrud "Ace" Steinman, was sixty-five. But she sure

didn't act like it. Ace cracked jokes non-stop when I interviewed her. She had twice as much energy as me on the best of days. The Oldtymers were happy to let me shoot video as they played shinny at the ponds.

"They're not *that* great," muttered Marty under his breath. He was obviously jealous of their skills and the attention I was giving them.

"I heard that, young man!" yelled Ace from the ice. "Would you care to join me on the ice for a little one-on-one shinny?"

Marty was never one to turn down a challenge. "You're on!"

I made sure the camera was rolling. Marty was in his usual fine form, swerving to and fro on the ice with perfect control. The cocky smile on his face said everything. He *knew* he was the best and he wasn't afraid to let everybody know it.

That smile didn't last very long though. Ace was the fastest skater I'd ever seen. She proceeded to take the puck from Marty at every opportunity. She skated circles around him. Her nickname "Ace" was well-deserved. I realized I was watching a living legend in action.

Marty tried playing harder, but it wasn't enough to even out the match. Ace made it look effortless as she zigzagged in a blur around him.

After ten minutes on the ice, Marty was huffing and puffing as though he'd run a marathon. Ace had barely broken a sweat. Like a rusty bike with loose wheels, Marty skittered off the ice and collapsed into the snow. It was kind of sad actually.

"I . . . stand . . . corrected," wheezed Marty.

"Apology accepted," replied Ace. "People always underestimate us because of our age."

"You really showed him, Grandma!" said Lise.

I turned to Lise. Had I heard her correctly? "Grandma?"

"Yep," Lise replied proudly. "Ace is our mom's mom. Who do you think taught Marty how to play hockey?"

12

THE GREATEST GIFT

I texted with Jackson almost every day. I told him all about life in Berksburg. He couldn't imagine living "in the middle of nowhere" and he had a lot of strange questions.

JACKSON: Do you hunt in the wild for fresh meat or do you have a supermarket in town?

ME: We have one small grocery store. They sell meat. Much easier than hunting.

JACKSON: Do you have electricity?

ME: Yep. (I wondered if Jackson realized it was the twenty-first century, even in Berksburg.)

JACKSON: What do you guys do for fun since you don't have a movie theatre in town?

ME: We play hockey. And we talk about hockey. And we talk about playing hockey.

I told Jackson all about my documentary, which he thought was a really cool idea.

JACKSON: Don't forget about me when you move to Hollywood! And if you ever need an actor for one of your blockbusters, remember to call me!

Later that night, Jackson sent me a link to a new photo he'd posted on Instagram. It was a picture of him standing in front of Old Man Chan's seafood market. He had a fish in each hand and he was making them kiss for old time's sake. "Wish you were here" was the message that went along with the photo. It made me smile, but it also made me miss Chinatown. I wondered who he'd gotten to take the picture. I also wondered how far Old Man Chan chased him down the street this time.

Shooting my documentary helped me forget about my homesickness. Soon the project became an obsession. I spent every spare moment with Dad's video camera firmly in hand. News spreads like wildfire in a small town like Berksburg, and before I knew it, people were asking me to include them in the documentary.

At school one day, I started talking with a classmate named Eric Johnson. He told me about how much his family loves hockey and its history.

"My grandpa says that Indigenous people like us should be proud because we helped to create hockey," he said. "The First Nations were playing games on the ice before Europeans settled here."

I didn't know that. Everyone seemed to have a different story about how hockey was born.

Some thought it was a form of an old Irish game called "hurley." Others thought it started in the Netherlands during the 1600s. Some people thought that Nova Scotia was the birthplace of modern hockey. Others thought it was Montreal or Northern Ontario. Nobody knew for sure how the game was actually invented.

Eric suggested that I interview his great-grandfather William, who was something of a legend in the area. At the ripe old age of 103, he was in amazing health and he still enjoyed jogging every morning. William was eager to share stories about growing up with hockey in Eastern Canada. I visited Eric's house on the outskirts of town where William lived in the basement.

The word "basement" hardly did justice to his living space. It was more like a museum full of artifacts passed down to him through the generations. One thing was clear the minute you entered his domain — hockey meant everything to him.

"Hockey is much more than a game," he told me in his slow but strong voice. "It's magic."

Eric just smiled and shook his head. "Great-Grandpa gets a bit carried away sometimes."

I quickly powered up the video camera and began recording William. I knew this was going to be good.

"What do you mean when you say it's magic?" I asked.

"Hockey brings people together. It can bring out the best in people. Courage. Teamwork. Honour. It requires many skills. Skating. Handling the puck. Heroes are born of hockey. It's more than a game."

William explained how he had learned to carve hockey sticks from curved tree roots. Scattered around the room were a number of sticks he'd carved over the years. He also had a number of wooden hockey pucks that were

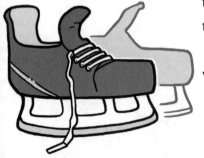

used in the early days of the game.

Hanging on the walls were framed, black and

white photos of young First Nations hockey players in uniform.

"That's me," he said, pointing to the tallest and biggest player in one of the pictures. "I used to play in one of the eastern Aboriginal leagues. I was great at keeping the puck, but my size kept me from skating as fast as some of the younger fellas. When I moved to Berksburg, I started my own team in town. All Indigenous players."

William's love of hockey came through in every word and his passion was contagious. He was a human encyclopedia of obscure facts about local hockey history. I could see why he was a local legend.

Before I knew it, I'd been there for hours and it was time to head home.

"Thank you for taking the time to help me with my documentary," I said, shaking his strong hand.

"It was my pleasure, young man," said William. "But before you go, I think you should take something with you. Eric tells me that your grandmother lives with you."

"That's right," I replied. "In our basement, kind of like you."

"Eric also tells me that she's having trouble adjusting to life here."

"You could say that."

William handed me a hockey stick. It was one that he'd carved out of a tree root, probably before my parents were even born.

"Please give this to your grandmother. It's a reminder that she's always welcome here in Berksburg and she's never alone."

For the first time, I truly felt the magic of hockey. It was the magic of bringing people together. I thanked William and Eric, and I told them they were always welcome to drop by for a visit.

That evening, I gave Po Po the hockey stick and told her what William had said. She cried. That made me cry. I could never let Jackson know that I was such a softy. I had a reputation to keep!

13
ADVENTURES IN EDITING

Editing. It's one of the scariest words in the English language. If you've ever tried to edit a video of any kind, you know what I mean.

Shooting a video is like gathering the ingredients for a recipe. Editing is like mixing those ingredients together, tossing them in the oven, and hoping that something decent comes out at the end.

"Anthony!" came Dad's frustrated yell from downstairs. "Are you still using my laptop? I need to use it once in a while too!"

True, I was hogging the laptop. I needed it for the editing software. I hoped Dad would come to realize that it was for a worthy cause.

"I just need it for another hour!" I yelled back from my room. "Or two." That last part was in a voice too soft for him to hear.

I started reviewing my video footage and taking note of the best parts. My filmmaking adventures had allowed me to meet some interesting characters. They each had unique reasons for loving hockey. Besides the folks I've already mentioned, some of the people I interviewed included:

- Mayor Edward Ulysses III. He was 110 per cent committed to making Berksburg the tourism capital of Ontario. It had been his obsession since his Kindergarten days. He didn't know how he'd increase the tourist trade in town (which was pretty well non-existent), but he wasn't giving up any time soon. Oh, and he was also obsessed with hockey. You probably already guessed that.

- Hazel Smithson. She had a neat collection of food items that looked like famous hockey players. Potato chips. Crackers. Even pancakes. She preserved them with varnish. My favourite was her prized Christmas cake, which she thought was the spitting image of Gertrud "Ace" Steinman. Personally, I didn't see it, although the raisins and cherries on her "face" looked yummy.

- Big Al. Didn't seem to have a last name. If he did, nobody knew what it was, himself included. He claimed to have been abducted by a UFO in the 1970s. Apparently the UFO resembled a giant hockey puck. Big Al believed that aliens created the game of hockey for the good of the universe.

- Ana Rohl. She was known as the Animal Lady because of the many pets living in her tiny house. She had three dogs, a dozen cats, five hamsters, and a pot-bellied pig. She made hockey uniforms

MAYOR EDWARD ULYSSES III

HAZEL SMITHSON

ANA ROHL

WILLIAM JOHNSON

for all of them and her hamster cage was decorated to look like a hockey arena, complete with tiny scoreboards. She was awesome beyond words.

- Rocky Dunleavensworthski. He ran a hockey-themed mini-golf course on the outskirts of Berksburg. He didn't give you putters to play with — he gave you hockey sticks. And instead of balls, you used pucks. They didn't actually fit into the holes on the course, so it was tough to keep score.

I didn't know where to start with my editing! The thought of sifting through hours of footage was really overwhelming. Whenever I tried to get started, my brain would freeze with fear.

I've always been good at putting things off when I don't want to do them. Instead of editing,

I found myself watching movies, playing video games, or cleaning my room! Even watching old videotapes of Chinese soap operas with Po Po seemed like a good alternative. Zero progress was being made.

My phone buzzed. It was Jackson texting again. Good. Another distraction.

JACKSON: How goes the editing?

ME: Not good. I can't get started. It's too scary and I don't know where to begin.

JACKSON: I know what you mean. I feel like that all the time with my homework.

ME: This is harder than I expected. Maybe I wasn't cut out to be a filmmaker.

JACKSON: You can do this. Just start with the part that's the most fun. It usually works for me.

I took Jackson's advice and began the dreaded process of assembling the documentary. I started editing all of the scenes that involved Lise because she always made me smile. Then I edited interviews with some of the wackier residents of Berksburg. I got a good laugh reviewing footage of Hazel Smithson and her watermelon that was shaped like her favourite NHL goalie.

The next few weeks of editing flew by. Putting my film together ended up being a lot of fun! I texted Jackson to thank him for his good advice.

Four weeks after I started editing, the documentary was complete. It was fifteen minutes long. I found it hard to cut out so much stuff. But I figured it was better to have a good video that's short rather than a boring video that's long.

Coming up with the right title was a challenge. Some of my ideas included:

1. *Berksburg: Where Everything Revolves Around Hockey and You Can't Escape It No Matter How Hard You Try*
2. *What's the Big Deal About Hockey Anyway?*
3. *Stick with It! The Berksburg Story*
4. *Have an Ice Day*
5. *Is Hockey for a Chinese Kid Like Me?* (That one was the worst.)

I eventually settled on the title *Berksburg: A Portrait of a Town and its Hockey*.

14

OPENING NIGHT

I wanted to show my film to Po Po before anyone else. I was surprised to see how excited she got when I told her it was finished. Po Po rarely got excited about anything other than her Chinese soap operas.

We settled in front of the laptop with a big bowl of popcorn and the lights down low. It was important to have the right mood for the premiere, even if it was only at the kitchen table.

"Let's get started," she said. "I'm not getting any younger! I want to see what this town is all about!"

I understood why she was so anxious. After all these weeks, she still hadn't ventured out of the house. My film was her chance to experience Berksburg for the first time. Even though Po Po had wanted to see my raw footage, I wouldn't let her see anything until the whole thing was completed to my satisfaction.

"Hey! Are you guys watching the video?" It was Mom. She could sneak up on you like a ninja.

"Yeah, Mom, but I was hoping to show Po Po first . . ."

"HONEY!" she yelled to Dad. Based on the ear-shattering volume of her voice, he was hanging out on the other side of the earth. "ANTHONY'S PLAYING HIS VIDEO!"

Dad soon arrived. The private screening for Po Po was turning into a family affair.

"Did someone say that Anthony's playing his video?" It was Chloe. And her entire English study group. That meant most of her class. There weren't even enough chairs in the house for the mob that had gathered in the kitchen.

"Is anybody else expected to arrive?" I asked sarcastically. "Or can I *finally* start the screening?"

"I'm glad we arrived on time!" It was Lise, Marty, and Buck.

I was starting to feel self-conscious. "Should we invite the Prime Minister too?"

"No, but you can have the next best thing!" It was Mayor Edward Ulysses III.

"But why are you . . .? Never mind. I'm starting the video NOW!"

And so I did. The documentary unfolded on the laptop screen and I translated for Po Po every time someone spoke. The film began with a short walking-tour of the town, much like the one I took during my first weekend in Berksburg. The narrator talked about the town's history and the importance of hockey to the community. Actually, *I* was the narrator. I'd lowered my voice as much as possible to sound older and more important.

Then the narrator started to introduce the colourful characters of Berksburg. Every time someone new appeared on screen, the entire kitchen would erupt into applause. Like I said, everybody knew everybody in Berksburg.

Watching the documentary with an audience for the first time was a really strange experience. It ended up being a lot funnier than I expected it to be. Everyone seemed to love watching Gertrud "Ace" Steinman skate circles around Marty. The interview with William about First Nations history and the magic of hockey was quite emotional.

Then it was over. The credits rolled and complete silence filled the room. I couldn't tell if it was a good sign or not.

"What did everyone think?" I asked. I was almost afraid of the answer I'd get.

Everyone looked shocked. Nobody seemed willing to speak up first. Not a good sign. Was the film really that bad? I felt like running and hiding under a rock.

Then someone started clapping. Followed by someone else. Soon everyone was clapping. Then people were on their feet. It was a standing ovation! I was getting hearty slaps on the back. Slaps, along with hugs, handshakes, and more compliments than I'd ever received in my entire life. Some people were even in tears.

Lise was clapping so wildly that her hands must have been getting sore. Marty was cheering as though his favourite hockey team had just won the championship. Buck was too busy eating his bag of chips to do much else. I think he looked impressed, but it was always hard to tell with him. He didn't have many facial expressions.

A huge smile was plastered on the mayor's face. It reached from ear to ear. It was kind of creepy actually.

"We're gonna be rich!" he said. "RICH! We'll be the biggest tourist attraction this side of Timbuktu!"

I wasn't sure where Timbuktu was, and I

wasn't sure that it was a big tourist attraction on the best of days. But I didn't say anything. At least he was happy.

I looked over at Chloe to get her reaction. She nodded at me with the proudest of smirks. Then she gave me a firm thumbs-up. Mom and Dad were hugging each other and twirling around in a dizzying fashion.

More than anything, though, I wanted to know what Po Po thought. She was still staring at the computer monitor, unblinking. Then she turned to me, kissed my forehead, and gave me one of her rarely-seen (toothless) smiles. I was reminded of a jack-o'-lantern I carved a few years back.

"Good job," she said as she fought back tears. "Now I'm ready to see Berksburg for myself."

I could barely believe my ears. I never thought my video could have such an effect on anyone.

"Now I can see that there's nothing to be afraid of," she continued. "I think your mother and father made a wise decision to move here. It looks like lots of good people live in Berksburg. When can you give me a tour?"

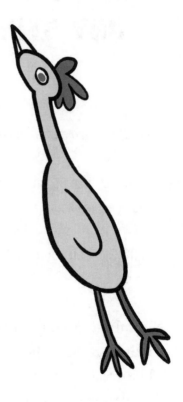

15

JUST WHEN I THOUGHT THINGS COULDN'T GET ANY STRANGER . . .

JACKSON: How did the screening for your grandma go?

ME: Better than I could've imagined! I can't believe how much people liked it.

JACKSON: Can you post it online? I'd really like to see it.

I'd never thought of sharing my documentary online because I didn't expect it to be any good. The great reaction at the screening changed my mind though. I posted it on YouTube that night so Jackson could watch it.

The next morning it was time to give Po Po her big tour of Berksburg. She was all ready to go at the crack of dawn, but I wanted to sleep for a bit longer. Po Po pounded on my door at 9:00 a.m. to wake me up. I tried to block the noise with a pillow over my ears, but it was no use. Time to start the day. Grrrrr.

I didn't even have a chance to eat breakfast. Po Po kept rushing me so we could start our adventure. She was so excited that she yanked me out the front door before I could even zip up my coat.

"Berksburg is prettier than I thought it would be," she said. We marched down the road, her arm clasped tightly around mine. It was obvious that she was still a bit nervous about being outside of the house. "I wonder if we'll see any wildlife."

I purposely didn't tell her about Clark the coyote. I didn't want to make her more anxious.

We walked downtown where several people said hello as they passed us. Po Po was too shy to say anything back, but she smiled and nodded. I could feel her hold on my arm starting to loosen.

Soon we reached the ponds where the regular crowd (most of the town) had gathered for games of shinny. We met Lise, Marty, and Buck, who were lacing up their skates at our usual spot.

"Hi guys," I said. "I brought a special person with me this morning."

"Good morning, Mrs. Peng!" they said. They looked surprised to see Po Po at my side.

"Good morning," she replied in Chinese. "And please call me Po Po instead of Mrs. Peng. You're all a part of my new, bigger family here in Berksburg."

I translated for my friends.

"That would be our honour, Po Po," said Lise.

Word had spread like wildfire throughout Berksburg about the screening of the film. A small crowd soon gathered around us. People wanted to hear about my cinematic master-piece. It felt strange but nice being the centre of attention for something other than falling on my bum.

"I wish I was there to see it!" said Eric.

"I'd like to see it too!" said Ace.

"I'm hungry!" said Buck.

"I posted it on YouTube," I told everyone. "Check it out and let me know what you think."

I introduced Po Po to everyone and she was greeted with friendly handshakes.

"Would your grandma be interested in join-ing us on the ice?" asked Ace. "I brought an extra pair of skates."

It was hard to imagine Po Po doing *any* kind of physical activity, much less playing shinny. When I translated for Po Po, her face lit up. She said "yes" right away.

"Are you sure this is a good idea?" I asked Ace. "I don't want her to fall down and break any bones."

"Don't worry," said Ace. "I have a couple of pylons in my car she can use for balance. I just want to get her involved."

I asked Po Po if she wanted a pylon.

"Of course not!" she replied. "I can handle myself."

Po Po laced up the skates and took to the ice. To my amazement, she was steady and graceful on her blades. She skated for several minutes before taking a break.

"I didn't know you could skate like that!" I said.

"She's a natural, no doubt about it!" came a voice from behind. It was William. I hadn't seen him since the day he'd given me the hockey stick for Po Po. "Anthony, will you please introduce me to this lovely young lady?"

I translated as William and Po Po said hello to each other — William in English and Po Po in Chinese. They really seemed to hit it off despite the language barrier. Both of them were blushing like nervous kids on a first date.

Was romance even possible between two people so ancient? What a weird day.

"It's never too late to fall in love," said Lise. "Isn't romance wonderful?"

"Yuck," said Marty. "I'm going back on the ice."

"Romance *is* wonderful," said Buck. "That's what makes the world such an amazing place. Love."

"I agree with Marty," I said. "YUCK!"

Buck went back to eating his chips.

Po Po had a huge smile on her face during the whole walk home.

"You're a good boy," she told me. That was totally unexpected. "Thank you for making an old lady feel young again."

I didn't know what to say. I just smiled and gave her a hug.

We were barely through the front door when Chloe ran down the stairs to greet us.

"It's gone viral!" she yelled. She sounded like someone who'd just won a million bucks.

"What are you talking about?" I asked. "Have you been into the energy drinks again?"

"Your documentary's gone viral!" she explained. "Everyone's talking about it on social media! You've had about a zillion views since you posted it on YouTube!"

Chloe wasn't kidding. My video was trending on social media and everybody seemed to love it. Several online newspapers had already written reviews and they were glowing.

"This is a talented young filmmaker who has a bright future ahead of him," wrote one reviewer.

"Anthony Chung's wonderful documentary is an emotional exploration of hockey's importance to Canadians," wrote another.

Jackson texted to congratulate me for becoming an Internet sensation.

JACKSON: Your film is awesome! The whole school's talking about it!

ME: I'm still in shock about the whole thing. This is happening so fast.

JACKSON: Do you know about the film festival here in

JUST WHEN I THOUGHT THINGS COULDN'T GET ANY STRANGER . . .

Toronto? It's called the Young Filmmakers of Excellence Film Festival. You should send in your documentary. Judges will pick the top ten films and they'll screen them at the Film Festival Theatre next month.

I wondered to myself — *does my film even have a chance of making the top ten?* I didn't want to get my hopes up and be disappointed.

JACKSON: They give the Golden Projector Award to the director of the best film. That could be you!

That night at the dinner table, I told my family about my conversation with Jackson.

"What does everyone think?" I asked. "Should I send in my documentary?"

"Only you can decide that," said Mom.

"We'll support you no matter what you decide," said Dad.

"Of course you should do it!" said Chloe. "If you don't, you'll regret it for the rest of your life!"

"I don't know . . ."

"If you don't enter this festival, I'll break your arm!"

"Give me some time to think about this. I don't want to rush into anything," I told her. "This is overwhelming. I need to give it some serious thought."

Twenty seconds later, I'd made my decision.

"I'm in! Film festival, here I come!"

16

WAITING FOR AN ANSWER

I submitted my documentary through the film festival's website. Uploading the video file, I was putting my work into the hands of the judges so they could decide my fate. It was nerve-racking to think that the jury of a real film festival was going to see my work.

Now it was a waiting game. What would they think of it? Would they like it as much as the people of Berksburg did? Would they laugh my film out of the competition? The suspense was killing me.

Knock. Knock. Dad poked his head into my bedroom.

"Did you submit your documentary yet?" he asked.

"Yep," I answered. "Just did it."

"Good. Just checking."

Then he was gone.

Knock. Knock. Mom poked her head into my bedroom.

"Did you hear anything back from the film festival yet?" she asked.

"Nope," I answered. "I just submitted it a couple of minutes ago."

"Good. Just checking."

Then she was gone.

Patience. I repeated that word in my mind over and over.

Knock. Knock. Chloe poked her head into the bedroom.

"Hey there," she said. "Did you hear any-thing . . .?"

"No I didn't!"

"Sorry I asked!" She slammed the door shut behind her.

Patience, Anthony. My inner voice was

starting to sound anything *but* patient.

Knock. Knock.

"For Pete's sake!" I yelled. "Who is it now? The Queen of England?"

Another head poked into my room. I was close. It was Mayor Ulysses III.

"Hello there, young man," he said. "I, Mayor Edward Ulysses III, can officially speak on behalf of the town when I say that we're all rooting for you. In fact, your documentary could really boost the tourism industry of Berksburg and . . ."

Blah blah blah blah blah. I started to tune him out.

Why hadn't I heard back from the film festival yet? Did they successfully receive my online submission? What if the website wasn't working properly? Or maybe the Internet connection was screwy?

I told myself to stay calm. There was no need to panic — yet.

A week passed. I still didn't hear anything from the festival. I was tempted to send them a polite email to ask, "WHAT'S TAKING SO FREAKIN' LONG?!!!!!!" Luckily, I let Lise talk me out of doing that.

I tried not to think about it, which was easier said than done. Ever since the video went viral, people around town started asking me for my autograph. That felt so unreal. Internet sites started contacting me for interviews. A Toronto news station even sent a video crew to shoot a story about my new-found fame.

I couldn't understand why anyone would be interested in writing about me or putting me on TV. I was just a kid who made a video that people happened to like. The whole situation seemed silly. How could I take my instant fame seriously when I still had homework to do?

Normal life dragged on as I waited for a response from the film festival. Po Po held another tai chi lesson the following weekend and everyone had fun. Old William had since joined the lessons and he was a natural. Lise and Marty were really getting the hang of it. Buck wasn't getting much better, but at least he wasn't falling over any more.

"I'm having fun teaching tai chi," Po Po told me. "Do you think anybody else in town would be interested in learning? Maybe this could be a new business for me!"

We were all relaxing after the lesson when my cell phone dinged. A new message.

"It's an email from the film festival!"

Everything in the room suddenly went silent (except for Buck, who was opening a new bag of chips). It was the moment of truth.

"We're proud of you no matter what they say," said Lise. She smiled her calm, reassuring smile.

"That's right," agreed Marty. "And besides, who cares what other people think?"

Buck nodded in agreement as he crunched away.

I took a deep breath and touched open the email.

"Thank you for your submission to our film festival," the message read. "Your film was selected as one of the top ten submissions. It will be screened at the Festival Theatre and it is officially in competition for the top prize. Congratulations."

I didn't have to say a word. Everybody could tell from my smile that it was good news.

The entire room erupted into applause. I was hoisted up onto everyone's shoulders like the hero I was. (To be honest, I *wasn't* hoisted up onto anyone's shoulders. But *I'm* the one telling the story, so let me exaggerate a little. I think I deserve it.)

Lise gave me a big hug, which was nice. Marty slapped me on the back so hard I thought my molars would fly out of my skull. Buck even stopped eating so he could shake my hand. He got chip grease and salt all over my hand, but that was okay. Then he knocked over a vase by accident. Luckily, Po Po hated that one too.

I texted Jackson right away to tell him the exciting news.

JACKSON: Awesome, dude! This is gonna make you so rich and famous!

ME: Let's not get carried away.

JACKSON: Seriously. It's the biggest festival for young filmmakers in Canada! And you're already an Internet sensation. You'll be moving to Hollywood before you know it! Can I come to the screening in Toronto?

ME: You bet! It'll be great to see you again. I've got so many neat stories to tell you about Berksburg!

PO PO'S TAI CHI CLASS TAKES OFF

17

FEELING LIKE A ROCKSTAR

I don't know how Mayor Ulysses III arranged such a big event on such short notice. I found myself at the Berksburg Arena a few nights later, being presented with the Key to the City at centre ice. It looked like the whole town had turned out.

"Welcome, ladies and gentlemen," said the mayor into the mic. With his glittery silver tuxedo and top hat, he was glowing — literally. And he was loving his big moment in the spotlight. "We are all proud to be from Berksburg — the hockey capital of the universe! This is a day that generations will remember and cherish!"

My family and I sat in a row of folding chairs beside the podium on a red carpet sprinkled with (fake) rose petals. I should have worn long underwear. My knees were getting chilly.

Mom and Dad looked really proud. Chloe was enjoying the attention from the crowd. Even Po Po was all smiles. Her misty breath rose from her toothless maw like a simmering volcano. A *happy* simmering volcano at least.

My bum was cold.

"We are here today to honour a true Canadian hero," the mayor continued. Boy, he wasn't holding back. "Mr. Anthony Chung, please approach the podium."

My jeans were frozen to the metal chair but I managed to break free with a slight twist. As I approached the podium, I could see Marty and Lise in the stands to my right. Buck was there too, but he was sleeping.

"Mr. Chung," said the mayor (all choked up), "I now present you with the Key to the City."

The place went nuts with

cheering. People were doing the wave. Air horns were blasting. Dozens of balloons were released from a net overhead. The mayor would have preferred *hundreds* of balloons instead of *dozens*, but he had a limited budget.

I took a close look at the Key to the City. It was a cheap-looking plastic key glued to a hockey puck. Someone had used a label gun to add the words "Berskburg Keye to the City" along the bottom. Despite the typos, I was genuinely touched.

Then the big event was over and we had to clear centre ice so the Zamboni could do its job. Nobody wanted the hockey game to run late!

After the big ceremony, I asked Marty and Lise to teach me how to play hockey. Now that I'd made a whole film about Berksburg and the game, I could see that hockey wasn't just a silly waste of time. It was an honoured tradition that brought the whole town together. It was a part of what makes Canada so special. Maybe hockey *was* for a Chinese kid like me.

Marty and Lise were happy to teach me how to play. At the ponds, they gave me tips on how to skate without falling over. They showed me how to shoot the puck without letting go of the stick. Progress was slow, but we were all having fun.

Eric brought some jerk-chicken wonton soup from Golden Egg Roll so we could warm up during our break. We took seats on our favourite log and enjoyed defrosting for a while. Then we cracked open our fortune cookies and pulled out the little strips of paper.

"What does your fortune say?" Eric asked Lise.

"It says that I have the best friends in the world," she replied.

"Mine says that I have good taste," said Marty. "A smart cookie!"

"My fortune says that I'll become rich someday," said Eric. "Sounds good to me!"

"Mine says that good luck is just around the corner," I said. "Let's hope that's true."

Soon, we were back on the ice to continue my hockey lesson. My feet were getting cold, so I started skating back to the riverbank to get an extra pair of socks from my backpack.

That's when I saw Clark the three-legged coyote grab the backpack in his mouth. When I shouted at him to stop, he dashed off into the forest like a bolt of lightning. I chased him as well as I could on skates (since there wasn't time to change into my boots).

Even though Clark had only three legs, he was way faster than me. I soon lost sight of him in the brush. The blades of my skates kept getting stuck in the ground, which slowed me down even more. I stumbled through the trees for several minutes trying to catch sight of him, but I didn't have much luck.

With my tail tucked between my legs, I returned to the ponds empty-handed. To my surprise, old William was chatting with Lise, Marty, and Buck. And at William's side was Clark "The Thief" himself on a leash. My bag was nowhere to be seen though.

"Howdy!" said William as though nothing was wrong.

"Hello, sir," I managed to say through my

confusion. "What's the coyote doing here?"

"Coyote?" replied William. "This isn't a coyote! This is my dog, Clark! He *does* look a bit like a coyote though, doesn't he?"

I told William about Clark taking my backpack.

"Sorry about that," the elderly man said. "He likes to take things and bury them in the forest. I hope there wasn't anything too valuable in your backpack."

"Just a bit of homework," I replied. "Hopefully my teacher will believe me when I tell her a coyote — er, a dog — buried it in the forest."

I couldn't stay angry at Clark, though. He was just too cute. When I looked into his big brown eyes, I could see how sorry he was.

That evening, I decided to give my film production "company" a name so it seemed more official. I settled on "Clark the Coyote Productions" after my new three-legged friend.

As of this writing, the bag and my extra socks are still missing in action.

18

BIG FISH
IN A BIG POND

The film festival was only a few days away. I'd never been so nervous in my life. What would audiences think of my documentary when it was screened in Toronto? What if they booed at the screen or started throwing tomatoes?

BAAAANG! I jumped. Was that a gunshot? Was it hunting season in Berksburg? Were gangsters trying to get me?

It turned out to be a backfiring engine. I hadn't heard that sound since the days of non-stop traffic in Chinatown. An old bus came to a stop in front of our house. Half the neighbourhood was already out there to see what was causing the racket. The bus was covered in rust and it looked like it could fall apart at any time.

But the strangest thing about the bus was the giant face painted on its side — *my* face! Whoever painted it had done a pretty good job, although my ears were too big. Also painted on the bus were the words "Clark the Coyote Productions" and a picture of my canine friend.

The bus door creaked open and out stepped Lise and Marty. I wondered where Buck was. (Hopefully he wasn't still asleep at the arena.) In the driver's seat was Mayor Ulysses III, who gave me a friendly wave.

"What do you think of the bus?" asked Lise. "Isn't it great?"

I didn't know what to say.

"You can thank *me*," said Marty proudly. "This was all my idea."

"I don't get it," I said. "What's this bus for?"

"You didn't think you were going to that film festival on your own, did you?" asked the mayor. "Half the town wants to go. And I'll be the driver! I bought this bus years ago and I used to live in it. But let's not get into that. I patched it up over the past few days."

One of the rear tires exploded.

"Don't worry," said the mayor without losing a beat. "I always carry a spare. Does anyone here know how to change a bus tire?"

The big day finally came. We would be on our way to Toronto at the crack of dawn. That way we'd have time to do some sightseeing before the next day's big screening. With so many people from Berksburg going to the festival, we

reserved an entire floor of a hotel downtown. The hotel was managed by the mayor's second cousin's best friend's neighbour. We got an amazing group rate.

Our car led the way and the bus followed with the mayor at the wheel. I was still nervous about the bus falling apart, but it was too late to do anything about it.

Lise, Marty, and Buck were really excited about the trip. None of them had been on a long bus trip before, and none of them had been to Toronto either. I was looking forward to showing them around my old hometown.

It felt weird leaving Berksburg for the first time since I'd arrived. I'd grown very fond of the town and its folks. Even though I was excited to visit the big city again, I felt sad seeing our house grow smaller and smaller in the rear-view mirror. I waved goodbye to the fake chicken over the door.

As we neared the Greater Toronto Area, traffic kept getting heavier. The farms along the highway disappeared and were soon replaced by high-rise condos and shopping plazas. When the CN Tower finally became visible on the horizon, my phone started buzzing. Lise and Marty were sending me excited texts.

"I can see the CN Tower!!!!!" wrote Lise. In fact, she had more exclamation marks than I've chosen to include here, but I think you get the picture. "I've always wanted to see the CN Tower with my own eyes!"

As we entered the heart of the city, Dad made a point of driving through Chinatown.

"Welcome to my old neighbourhood!" I texted Lise.

I was so excited to be in Chinatown again. It was great to see all of the hustle and bustle. At the same time though, part of me missed the slower pace of life in Berksburg. Maybe I was actually becoming a bit "Berksburgian." (Or was it "Berksburgenish"?)

Our hotel was just a short walk from the glittering lights of the theatre district. The honking of horns and rustling of streetcars filled the air. Skyscrapers loomed overhead and blocked out the sky. Not that we would have seen stars anyway. It must have been quite the alien environment for my friends from Berksburg.

We checked into our rooms before setting out as a group to do some sightseeing. I led everyone down Yonge Street. The giant digital billboards around Dundas Square competed for our attention with street performers juggling and dancing for the entertainment of tourists. A few people actually recognized me and asked for autographs!

Then we made our way to Chinatown. I took everyone to Wong's Restaurant for the best Chinese food in the city. It was strange to see most of the seats in the place filled by people from Berksburg! Jackson met us at the restaurant and it was fun introducing him to my new friends. They seemed to click right away.

"Chinatown is amazing!" Lise told Jackson.

"Everything is so exciting here!" said Marty.

"Berksburg sounds awesome," said Jackson. "I'd like to visit someday."

We ordered some traditional Chinese dim sum, which most of my new friends had never tried before. Lise really enjoyed the shrimp dumplings. Marty preferred the steamed pork buns. Buck was brave and tried the chicken feet, which he actually enjoyed. Po Po looked like she was having fun ordering different dishes for William to try — she was so proud to be sharing her culture. It was nice to see Eric enjoying the food too.

To be honest though, I *did* miss some of the dishes from Golden Egg Roll. I'd grown really fond of their jerk-chicken wonton soup — a true Berksburg original.

Our next stop — the CN Tower! Our group was so big that it took several elevator trips to get us all to the observation level. As our elevator zoomed upward and the streets grew tinier below, Lise was shaking because she was so excited. Marty was afraid of heights, so he refused to open his eyes. Buck was smiling as much as Lise. But I couldn't tell if it was just because he was enjoying his bag of popcorn so much.

The view from the observation deck was magnificent in all directions. The tiny cars on the highway below looked like toys and the people on the sidewalks scurried about like ants. As we looked out to the misty lights of the Toronto Islands, Lise put an arm around my shoulder. I could feel my face turning red with embarrassment.

"Thank you for making one of my dreams come true," she said.

I just smiled and enjoyed the moment.

19

THE IMPORTANT THINGS IN LIFE

The Film Festival Theatre in downtown Toronto. We were actually here to see my film on the big screen! It felt like a dream.

I was dressed in a black suit that was a bit too tight for comfort. I hated getting dressed up. It felt very un-me. But Mom thought that no respectable filmmaker would show up to his premiere without a suit. Oh well — it made her happy. And I felt better when Lise said I looked like James Bond.

Lise was stunning in a dark blue dress that made her look like a movie star. Marty wore a black suit too. But he looked completely comfortable in his. Who would have expected that? Buck had refused to wear a suit, but he wore his best black T-shirt with his ripped jeans.

I took a deep breath. I tried to stay calm as we took our seats. A buzz of excitement filled the room. Young filmmakers from across Ontario were waiting for their films to screen.

The lights in the theatre dimmed and a spotlight focused on a gentleman at the podium. His tuxedo looked very expensive. With a white beard and tiny eyeglasses drooping down his nose, he looked like Santa Claus in a penguin suit. It was the celebrated film director Reginald P. Eggburt. He was also the founder and president of the film festival.

"Welcome to the Young Filmmakers of Excellence Film Festival," said Mr. Eggburt in his booming voice. "Ladies and gentlemen, we are honoured to have so many talented young artists in our midst tonight."

The entire audience erupted into applause. Some of that applause was for *me*!

"We received more than five hundred submissions from filmmakers all over Ontario," Mr. Eggburt continued. "Tonight, you will see the top ten films. But only one will walk away with the Golden Projector Award. So without any further delay, let the films begin!"

I'd been told that my documentary would be shown last. The order of the films was randomly drawn. Too bad my film couldn't go first so I could get it over with. Then I'd be able to relax and enjoy the rest of the evening.

The house lights were dimmed and the first film began to unfold on the screen.

I was amazed at how different the other films were from mine. Each one had its own unique style, but they were all fantastic. I was excited that my film was being shown along with the others. But I was also feeling a bit nervous. How could my little film about Berksburg compete with them?

The shortest of the films was only a minute long. It told the story of a girl and her guinea pig and used animated clay figures. The longest one was over twenty minutes long and it was a detailed history of cheese-making in the province. Buck later admitted that it was his favourite of the bunch. He loves cheese.

The films were screened one after another with no break between them. When the end credits of the ninth film starting rolling, I could feel my body tensing up. Sweat started rolling down the sides of my face. I felt a tremor throughout my body. My big moment was coming up.

The credits came to an end. Then, to my surprise, the house lights came up and Mr. Eggburt walked back to the podium. I was confused. Why weren't they showing my documentary?

"I hope you enjoyed watching all the films this evening," he said. He took a white envelope from his jacket pocket. "So without further delay, the winner is —"

"Wait!" It was Chloe. She was on her feet. For once I was glad she had the loudest voice in the world. "You forgot to screen the tenth film!"

Mr. Eggburt looked embarrassed. "I'm so sorry! You're absolutely right. Let's see the final film now, shall we?"

The lights were dimmed again. It was time for *Berksburg: A Portrait of a Town and its Hockey* to make its theatrical debut. As the film played on the big screen, I was surprised by how good it actually was. Maybe I *did* have some talent as a filmmaker after all.

Every time a new person from Berksburg appeared in the film, my friends and family cheered at the top of their lungs. Everybody seemed to be enjoying it, even people who weren't from Berksburg.

Fifteen minutes went by quickly and my documentary was over. As the applause died down, Lise leaned over and gave me a kiss on the cheek. That was the best part of the whole trip.

Mr. Eggburt returned to the stage. "I think we can agree that all ten films were outstanding," he said. "Congratulations to our finalists for their submissions. Unfortunately, we can pick only one film for the top prize."

He began to unseal the white envelope. This was the big moment.

"This year, the Golden Projector Award goes to . . ."

Mr. Eggburt struggled with the envelope. He couldn't quite get it open. The suspense was driving me bonkers! After what seemed an eternity, he finally managed to tear the thing open. He slid a piece of paper from the envelope and carefully unfolded it.

"I'm having trouble reading who the winner is," he said through squinting eyes. "Oh, that's why! I forgot my glasses backstage. Could someone please get them for me?"

Several tense moments passed before someone successfully retrieved Mr. Eggburt's glasses.

With his glasses once again perched upon his nose, Mr. Eggburt cleared his throat for dramatic effect. "This year, the Golden Projector Award goes to . . ."

I closed my eyes and took a deep breath.

". . . *A Detailed History of Cheese-Making in the Province* by Alice Togglethorne."

I felt deflated. But I was relieved at the same time. Of all the films, the one about cheese was my favourite. You can't beat a film about cheese-making. I realized the jury had made the right choice.

I didn't win the Golden Projector Award. But that didn't make me a loser. My film had just been screened alongside nine amazing films from some of the brightest young film-makers in Ontario.

Lise reached over and gave me a bear hug, squeezing the air from my lungs.

"Does anybody feel like going to Wong's Restaurant for dinner again tonight?" she asked. "I could go for some more shrimp dumplings."

"And I could go for some steamed pork buns," said Marty.

"I'm too full to eat any more," said Buck as he crumpled his empty popcorn bag. I could hardly believe my ears.

"Can I visit you guys in Berksburg?" asked Jackson. "It sounds like a cool place."

On our way to Wong's, I couldn't keep from smiling. This had been an incredible adventure. But I couldn't wait to get back home. Back to my life in Northern Ontario. Back to school, tai chi, and shinny with my friends. And back to filmmaking. I already had an idea for my next film. And it was going to be awesome!

ACKNOWLEDGEMENTS

Special thanks to Kat Mototsune, Laura Cook, Kean Soo, Derek Fryer, Darren Lampson, Michael Cordeiro, Vivienne Mathers, Ben Lam, Anna Lam, Ryan Lam, Franziska Boettcher, Moe Murphy, Shirley Murphy, Tina Maslakow, Jason Maslakow, Finley, and of course, the incomparable Erin Murphy and Laura Lam.